# Seppuku

## Issue V

# Seppuku

Seppuku/Joseph Fulkerson

ISBN: 979-8-9873315-3-8

Laughing Ronin Press

P.O. Box 234

Owensboro, Ky 42302

www.laughingroninpress.com

## sep·pu·ku /ˈsepo͞oˌko͞o, səˈpo͞oˌko͞o/

(Japanese: 切腹, "cutting [the] belly"), sometimes referred to as hara-kiri is a form of Japanese ritual suicide by disembowelment.

It was favored under Bushido (warrior code) as an effective way to demonstrate the courage, self-control, and strong resolve of the samurai and to prove sincerity of purpose.

# Note From The Editor

Starting with the fourth edition, I dropped the "Quarterly" moniker. The journal will henceforth be known simply as **"Seppuku."** It will still come out every quarter-ish and contain the same quality of writing you've all come to expect—As long as you continue to write quality pieces.

Thanks to all contributors both new and regular, as your engagement and passion make putting this journal together an absolute pleasure.

*Joseph Fulkerson*

# Numb

## Jake Kavanaugh

Megan still had her Hulu account on his TV. Letterkenny might have taken his mind off what demanded his attention. She would not mind since her mom paid for the subscription anyways. But she also couldn't mind because she was dead, Megan's friend had just called to tell him earlier that day. She was dead and he was watching Hulu that her mom paid for. He had been having a long day, hell he had been having a long week. He thought while sitting on the soft brown couch, still in his greasy work boots he did not bother to take off. Thoughts that started out slow sped up as he stared at the screen with a dry mind. He and Megan had left off at the previous episode and would not be back to continue. He was numb. That show was dumb. Maybe it wasn't the show she liked either, but she came over to lay on the couch with him and watched it. His old house had shitty heat and it would have been great to lay on the couch with her. His roommates were not home yet as the episode ended and he would have to tell them something. He was never that good with words. Glancing around the cluttered living room which was fading to darkness as the sun set behind the blinds. A slim can made its way across the room and into his mind. Megan was drinking from it at one point in time where the room wasn't so dim. It was time to get up.

# Sound and Silence

Ace Boggess


Owl-like noise of screeching from the ground,

a raccoon kit calls to its absent mother

as it walks a crude circle, road to yard

to road, repeat. Night fills

with the known sadness of loneliness,


loss. The mother will return,

no doubt—she always does,

however far alone she wanders

seeking food to fill a different void.

The kit is lost without her,


barely a bowl of fur with legs.

Like all the young, it has questions.

I'm sorry I can't answer them.

I stand nearby, calling to no one,

waiting for no one or nothing to reply.

# A Mountain No Longer Standing Tall

Luke Young

Once majestic

Rising towards the unattained clouds

Moisture laden in snow caps and glaciers

No one dreamed in ages past that dynamite alone could end you

Yet that is what has been done

Faded into old photographs

We'll now say "There used to be…"

# Spare the Rod

## Preacher Allgood

Some people tell you one thing. Other people tell you another thing. Some of its half lie and some of its half-truth and some of it could have been said in half as many words. You never remember what they said. But there are those times that someone says something that sticks with you the way infant possums' cling to mamma's back while she crawls under the barn door to get at the chicken feed.

My granddad said something that stuck with me. I was fifteen. He was in his seventies and a veteran of WWI. He'd lost one lung and half the roof of his mouth in a mustard gas attack. We were in his garage. It was gloomy and dank, and I was waiting for a beating and the ass chewing of a lifetime. He'd just witnessed me call my mother a bitch. I trembled and tried to hide it from him.

He reached behind a workbench, pulled out a pint of whiskey, unscrewed the cap, and took a swig. Then he handed me the bottle. I stared at him with my mouth open. I thought it was a trick. "Go ahead. Take a drink," he said. I did. It kicked the shit out of the back of my throat and then roiled my stomach. I bent over at the waist and spit and sputtered. It was all I could do to keep from puking.

"A good man never insults a woman," he said. "A smart man keeps his mouth shut whenever he can. Words are trouble. Silence is the cure. I hope you choose to carry yourself as a good and smart man." He recapped his bottle. Stuck it back in its place, and we left the garage.

That was fifty years ago. I never forgot it. I never will. And I imagine that old man, wherever he is, regrets sparing the rod every time I'm stupid enough to string another poem or another story down the page.

# Osaka Japan 1985 *Based on a true story*

**Missy Brownson**

A statue of Colonel Sanders stands

at the bottom of the Dōtonbori River,

string-tied and smiling, but mourning

the loss of his hand, left

cursing the local baseball team

who dropped him here,

as only a Kentucky Colonel can.

*Son of a biscuit*, he mutters.


He'd shake his fist,

if only he could.

# Dry Town

**George Anderson**


The guy in the Pathfinder
says he now knows why
his daughter works in Utopia

says I must have noticed
the police presence in Alice

how they have cops checking
IDs outside every liquor store.

He tells me the locals
can drink beer in the pubs

but it is the fortified wine
they are really after & how

they'll drive to Mount Isa
& back

800 kilometres each way-
to get it.

# *Prelude To A Wild Party*

**George Anderson**

Buds deeply suspicious
of the extended absence
of his partner Joy

climbs onto the rim of the bathtub
and peers through the porthole
to the adjoining toilet room below.

There they are: Tabarnac! The party
only an hour or two fucking old!

His girlfriend is bobbing
up & down on his good friend Andre
who is sitting on the can, his
mouth upwards, agape.

Buds leaps down from the tub
and rips open the toilet door
shattering the thick oak wood.

He grabs Joy by the neck
but she is out the door,
bolting headlong up Rue St. Jacques
through the pelting wet blizzard-

dodging cars. Buds in drunken pursuit.

# Salvation

## Kathleen Denizard

They came to witness the Salvation
Under a queer moon that reflected lantern lights and the glow
of cigarettes
Crusaders wailing in a thunder of psalms enticed them into a
communal circle
A believer danced about the tent feeling the boom of drums
inside him,
Stretching and flailing his arms upward as if to pull heaven
down,
Chasing and beseeching the spirits who might embrace him
Long slow breaths oozed the sweat from his body,
His tongue and lips burning in the heat of his ritual
Others came forward falling from the circle,
Writhing in furious motion, demonstrating their passion in
exhausting fervor
Presently smoke from the lanterns disappeared into darkness
Dancing figures slowed to a faint patter of drums
The incessant chanting silenced as if all blended into a single
trance
The Believer, shaken to his knees, stared at the ground

Now his voice, low and deliberate, sang out through the
congregation
  I'm saved!
  They believed

# Take Out

**Kathleen Denizard**

By the back porch
Sent out for it
Again

Stoop in the dim lit
Storm door entry
And grab the paper bag

It lay there delivered
Credit card approved
Tip included

Folded crisp and crinkled
The sound it made
Touching French fries and burger

Not the dinner for queens
Not an occasion for friends
Solitary meal

The sun going down

And candle at the table

My eyes to the television

# Worm Food

## Jack Moody

"I heard when your head's cut off you still have thirty seconds of consciousness before the brain dies. You just sit there with no body, blinking for half a minute." Danny prodded the severed head with his boot. "There's this account of some guy executed by the guillotine. While his head was in the little basket, someone said his name and his eyes opened, and he looked at the person who called him. He recognized his name."

Terrance danced around the pool of blood and reached into the body's pants pocket. He opened up the wallet and looked at the driver's license. "Hey. Hey, Mary? Mary! Wake up!" He whistled like commanding a dog to heel. "Right here. Hello."

Together they stared at the head. Danny frowned. "Maybe it doesn't always work." He surveyed the wreckage of the car crash: the shattered windows, the twisted metal, the skid marks, the caustic smell of skin and fat tissue fusing into leather seats. A solitary arm protruded from a jagged hole in the other car's windshield, erect and rigid as if it were waving at them. The rest of its body had flown through the open passenger window and disappeared somewhere in the cornfield on the side of the road. Physics is interesting like that.

"I think it needs to be a clean cut," said Terrance. He watched the blood and brain matter oozing from the eyes and nostrils. "She got bounced around too much. Damaged the brain stem. I bet that's what it is."

"Yeah. Maybe," Danny answered. "If she'd worn a seatbelt it might have sliced right through."

"Maybe. She'd have to have been going pretty fast though."

"Yeah."

The two men took turns frowning at Mary's unblinking head.

"Well," Terrance sighed, putting a cigarette to his lips. "Let's write it up. Cops'll be here soon."

* * *

"The experiment was bullshit. And MacDougall was a sadist. I thought we were trying to do something real here."

Danny looked out onto miles and miles of flat farmland as Terrance drove towards a three-car pileup along Route 66. The call had just come in over the police scanner, but it was a remote location and they were close, so the two men figured they'd have at least a five- or six-minute window to observe before the authorities arrived.

"We are. And he was too. Science isn't always gonna be pretty, Danny. Sometimes you have to get comfortable with a moral gray area to find progress."

"I don't care so much about the morality, okay? It was mostly for argument's sake."

"We're not arguing. We're having a discussion. Why was it bullshit? I wanna know why you think it was bullshit."

Danny waved at a herd of black and white cows grazing by the highway. "His whole deal began with the idea that animals don't even have souls. That's a presumptuous baseline. And how do you think he got the dogs? They didn't come in dying. He didn't just walk into a pet shelter and go, 'Hey. I need to kill some dogs, can I have some dogs that are already on their way out?' He poisoned healthy strays, strapping 'em to the table to measure the weight. That's sadism. That's sick, man."

Terrance was half-listening, his eyes narrow and focused on the road ahead, waiting for a glimmer of broken glass or a plume of smoke. "Okay, but that has nothing to do with whether the results were bullshit. Be objective, Danny. Put on your fuckin' big boy pants and be scientific about this. Where'd the 21 grams go?"

"Well first of all, none of that was conclusive. One patient lost weight at death but then lost even more weight. Another lost weight but gained the weight back. And he didn't even really bother to weigh the dogs properly at all. His mind was already made up before then: animals don't have souls.

That's bias. That alone should disregard the experiment entirely."

"But the third patient—"

"21.3 grams, yeah. But that could be anything. The organs are shutting down; sweat glands are opening up. It could have easily been 21 grams of sweat. He could have shit himself a little. There are lots of explanations. And there was no follow-up. No repeating of the experiment for a better conclusion. The guy was a hack and a fucking sadist."

"You just don't like that he hurt animals. That's bias too. You're still not being objective."

Danny followed a scattered group of sheep with his eyes. They were like little isolated bubbles of fog hovering over the field. "I'm *objectively* saying fuck that guy. We'll get better results—on people."

Terrance eyed his partner, gauging his mood before answering: "I'm just playing devil's advocate. You don't need to start fuckin' crying."

"I'm not." Danny squinted and pointed to a distant spot on the road. "There. Look."

Three cars sat smoldering across both lanes, crumpled into each other like a defective accordion. The middle car had the worst of it; a bright orange fire over the hood hissed and flickered in the wind. The windshield of the front car had been blown out and a streak of blood led to a body lying flat on the asphalt. The car at the back, presumably the instigating party, was still running; its engine revving like the driver was in shock and still pressing down on the gas pedal.

Terrance pulled to the side of the road. "Alright. Let's see what we can get. In and out—five minutes."

They approached the backmost car first. Its tires were squealing, unable to propel the vehicle farther into the trunk of its crumpled roadblock. The sweet smell of burning rubber floated from the scene.

Danny pressed his face against the driver's side window. The man was slumped over the steering wheel, his mouth agape, his eyes glazed over. Dribbles of blood ran down his temple "It's deadweight," he said. "His foot's stuck like a cement block on the pedal. He's long gone."

Terrance grunted. "Alright, next one then. Let's go, c'mon."

The center car was hardly recognizable as a vehicle that once ran. The back half had been crushed up to the center console like a turtle retreating into its shell. The woman inside was mangled beyond recognition; her head caved in and body twisted into an inhuman shape as if stuffed into a small box. Her arms and legs were shattered and bent in different directions across her chest.

"Don't bother," said Terrance. "She's a fuckin' pretzel. Next one."

Danny pointed to the third body lying a few yards away from the accident and whistled. It had evidently been thrown through the windshield upon impact. "That boy grew wings. Goddamn."

He jogged ahead while Terrance stopped to linger and stare at the woman's corpse, mumbling to himself something about the circus and contortionism.

Danny took a knee next to the man, and upon seeing that he was still breathing, felt his heart rate spike. "Hey. Hey, man." He shook the victim's shoulder—the one that wasn't relinquished of clothes and skin from skidding across the road—and he looked at Danny as if he were gazing up at an angel.

"Help me," he said. Blood poured over his broken teeth when he opened his mouth. Blood too drained from his left ear, and so Danny knew the hemorrhaging would cloud his mind soon, and death would quickly follow.

"*Three minutes,*" Terrance called over, his eyes still trained on the mess of skin, flesh and bone wedged between the center car's seat and dashboard. "*We got a live one or what?*"

He was a perfect candidate. They'd never found someone so within that rare, sweet spot between life and death. Danny fumbled his words when yelling over his shoulder, still staring into the man's eyes, watching the lights dim. "*Y—yeah. Hang on. Just hang on.*" He grabbed the man's chin, ignoring his plea. "Hey. Hey, focus. Look at me. What do you see right now?"

The man's expression was blank. He was in shock, or in awe, or too muddled to make sense of the situation. It was possible they'd missed the threshold where he could still comprehend language. But again, in a choked whisper, the man said, "Help me."

"Yeah, yeah. Yeah, I'm gonna help you. You're gonna be fine. But you need to tell me what's going on. You're dying right now. I need you to understand that and tell me what you're experiencing. Quickly now."

Danny realized he was leaning hard against the man's chest, because when his heart stopped the hollowness reverberated against his arm. The man's eyes opened wide. As if something had appeared. He inhaled and failed to let go of the breath within his lungs, as if he knew it was his last and refused the finality of its escape. The man reached a limp and broken arm to Danny's cheek and leaned in close to his ear. The words he spoke left his mouth with the exhalation, and after Danny fell backwards upon hearing them it was no longer a man who had spoken, but an empty body.

Terrance appeared from behind, peering at the corpse. "Did you get anything? Looked like he was wriggling around a bit. I figured he was too banged up though."

Danny turned around, hunched, sitting there at the center of the road, his stunned and pale face a vivid reflection of what he'd witnessed.

"Goddamn." Terrance grinned and laughed. "You look like you've seen a ghost."

* * *

When you're driving at night out in the middle of nowhere, and the streetlamps are few and far between, and the new moon hangs in the sky, you can begin to feel as though you're not moving at all. The world is empty and veiled by darkness and fog, and the only sign that you're alive at all is the passage of the yellow lines appearing at the dim ends of your headlights, until disappearing again beneath the wheels. It begins to feel like purgatory, like the illusion of movement, traveling nowhere forever.

Danny hadn't talked since they got back in the car. The words played over and over in his head, attaching to every thought like the roots of a poisonous plant.

"I didn't think you were this squeamish." Terrance had grown tired of the silence. "You've seen worse. You'll see worse. I thought we were in this together."

Danny remained stoic. Trance-like. Watching the yellow lines appear and disappear in the claustrophobic new world of fog and darkness. "We are," he answered. "We need more data."

"Did you get anything from the guy? You didn't write anything down. It's important we write everything down, even if it's not directly related to our hypothesis. We need to do this right. Okay? You gotta stay with me here. Don't get all loopy 'cause you saw a dead body."

"I'm not loopy," said Danny. "He was too far gone. Didn't know what he was saying. Nothing worth writing down. Worthless babble. That's all."

Terrance appraised his partner with a brief glance. "What did he tell you?"

"Gibberish. Just gibberish."

"Did you stick to the script?"

"Yes, man. I stuck to the fuckin' script. We just need more data. I need to talk to more people. We're moving too slowly. Our methods aren't conducive to—"

"Our methods are sound," Terrance interrupted. "We can't rush this. We gotta do this by the book."

"What fuckin' book?"

"It's a figure of speech. We can't let our own ideologies muddy the results. You need to be objective, Danny. Tell me what he said to you. Whatever it was obviously shook you up. I can't have you crashing this whole thing because a dying man with head trauma told you he saw the Devil or some shit. People are fucked up; they're gonna see a lotta different things. That's not what we're after here."

"Okay," Danny turned and glared into the side of Terrance's head, "then what *are* we after? Huh? What do *you* think we're gonna find? And what happens if it's something you don't wanna know?" When Terrance didn't respond, he repeated, "I need more data. Another subject."

Danny turned on the police scanner. He flipped between channels of white noise and minor infraction codes before an emergency responder rambled off a description and address in a monotone voice that juxtaposed harshly with the event's circumstances.

"How close are we?"

Terrance whipped his head between Danny and the scanner's blue glow. "What—*now*? Are you kidding? We don't do that. I won't. Car crashes and medical emergencies, no blatant crimes. That's the rule."

Danny ignored this and reiterated: "How close, Terrance?"

Terrance looked out the window for a street sign but didn't answer.

"What happened to being objective? This is prime. This is what we want."

"*Objective*?" Terrance snapped, his knuckles turning white against the wheel. "I could ask you the same fuckin' thing. That guy got you rattled. You're in no shape right now. And it's not close enough, alright? It'd be a mistake."

"Fine, then you get me nearby and drop me off. I'll observe by myself. Do both our jobs."

"You understand what you're asking me? You really wanna run that risk?"

"Yes, motherfucker." Danny tapped on the police scanner. "Clock's tickin.' You want the data or not? No—look at me. You want an answer?"

Terrance's eyes shifted between Danny and the rearview mirror, mumbling to himself before abruptly pulling a U-turn. "Hang on," he said. "We're gonna have to break a few laws."

The engine screamed as they disappeared farther into the nebulous fog, the highway's yellow lines the sole guide leading them through oblivion.

* * *

The front door had been left open. The lights of the all the surrounding houses were on, and a neighbor's dog was barking as if trying to warn Danny of what waited inside. There was no time; he understood and accepted that. It didn't matter. Nothing else mattered now but the words seared into his mind.

"In and out," said Terrance. "I mean it. I'll circle the block and you meet me outside in two minutes. Hey—" he snapped his fingers to get Danny's attention, "you hear me?"

"Yeah," he answered. He stepped out of the car and watched it turn right and disappear into the shadows beneath glowing streetlamps.

The door was blocked, stopping halfway with a soft thud. Danny squeezed through the space and found the lifeless body of a man. It was splayed across the welcome mat, its arms out. Like so many others its mouth was agape, as if his final breath had expelled with a scream. The pool of blood was still spreading across the hardwood floor, pouring from a small wound in its back. Its eyes were blue and milky with tears. The blood and the body were still warm. The man was very dead.

Across the room a dog sat whining on its haunches, wagging its tail, its ears pinned back in fear or confusion. Beside the dog lay the woman. Somewhere far enough away outside, the sound of police sirens approached. Danny stepped forward carefully, holding out the back of his hand towards the dog. He kneeled beside the woman. She'd missed the brain and had blown off the lower half of her jaw. Her tongue hung loosely through the hole in her face, resting atop the row of exposed bottom teeth. Her breathing was ragged and shallow, and her eyes followed Danny as he observed what she'd become. A nauseous mixture of blood-choked gurgles and hoarse squeals escaped her throat, and nothing more. The revolver lay beside her limp right hand. Its barrel was still hot to the touch.

"Hi," said Danny. He reached out to stroke the dog's head, and it leaned in closer, desperately needing the comfort of touch, whining but not barking. He wanted to take the dog away but knew it wouldn't yet leave. His empathy was reserved for the animal, and the empathy and worry it had for the woman was all she would receive. It was going to be a drawn-out death. Slow and painful.

"I'm going to ask you some questions," he said as calmly as he could. "You are dying. You may already know this. Or you may think that you will be saved. You will not. I need you to understand that fact before you answer the questions. Do you understand what I'm telling you?"

The woman's eyes grew large and her breathing became rapid and panicked. She formed the words that were still discernable but slurred as if spoken by a stroke victim: "Help me."

"I will," Danny replied. "First, answer this question. Knowing what you now know, tell me what you see. Tell me what you're experiencing. Think very carefully about this. Banish the idea of God or an afterlife or the actions of your past. Your answer requires objectivity. It will be the most important answer you will ever give. It will be your salvation—the truth."

Allowing the woman time to stare and scream inside her mind, Danny stroked the dog's head, kneading its ears. He took its collar in his hand and looked at the tag: "Charlie. Hi, Charlie. Good boy. You're a good boy."

Saliva and blood pooled beneath her tongue and spilled over her bottom lip. The sirens grew louder. A car screeched to a stop just outside the house.

"You're running out of time," he urged. "Quickly."

Terrance slammed the door against the body while trying to get in. "We gotta go," he shouted, and gazed down at the corpse, and at Danny kneeling before the woman.

Danny didn't turn, but continued staring into the woman's eyes, waiting. The distant glare of red and blue lights shined through the windows.

"Just leave her! Fuck it, man! C'mon!"

"Do you wanna hear something?" Danny whispered into her ear, jabbing his shoulder as Terrance grasped the back of his shirt. "I'll tell you what I know. But it doesn't have to be true. Remember that. It doesn't have to be."

He plucked the dead man's words from his mind, tearing each consonant and vowel off the walls as if they'd been stapled to the inside of his skull, fighting every instinct that howled for him to hide them away, and spoke softly, so softly, for only the woman to hear.

Her eyes turned to fire. Resurrected but for a moment. Unspeakable horror erupted from every nerve, and she so desperately tried to scream but what came was something unearthly. Not evil but a response to it. Blood drained from her face, her hair graying before his eyes, the skin melting away under the weight of revelatory visions. As if he had spoken the forbidden phrase to call upon the end of the world.

With such a force of strength that betrayed her frailty, the woman clasped both sides of Danny's head, thrusting him towards her. There were screams and movement, and the room had exploded with lights and life, but the woman spoke into his ear, and in that moment they were forever locked together, separate from the repercussions of any action, of history and time itself. Burrowed together beneath infinity, the woman spoke. The pieces of the universe unraveled like thin yarn. And Danny heard.

His mind shattered. Every perceived belief and moral and justification that had made him who he had become— hoarded and protected across a lifetime by the certainty of self— unfurled and dissolved. It was truth. The sequence of sounds uttered only once before, or only heard once before, and it was true. It was true. It was true. He had made a terrible mistake.

A different pair of hands, larger and gloved, pulled him by the collar. The revolver was in Danny's hand and it fired. The policeman fell. Another, and the sounds of Hell turned to the swan song of dying cells. Ringing. But still the words were there. The next man fell. A molten hot force struck his shoulder, and still it was nothing, it felt like nothing, not numbness, but something further within the abyss of that which should never be known. It had all been rendered meaningless. There was nothing.

Danny stood. The two policemen lay bleeding out, coughing, and Terrance lay on his stomach, handcuffed, and he said words but they were not the words of the woman, and so they were without sound. He aimed the pistol and fired, and it struck his partner in the head, and he turned to the woman, the oracle, the demon, or that which had instantaneously and briefly inhabited one, aimed, and fired. He collapsed on the ground, pressed the hot barrel against his temple, inhaling the scent of cauterizing flesh and pulled the trigger. And at the moment he heard the dull click, the words that swirled and became him like a cancer overtaking every cell, every molecule, rearranged before his eyes like a fantastic lightshow, and it was so funny. It was so fucking funny. The words burned through his eyes like a brand thrust into the cow, and it was—it was the greatest fucking joke he'd ever heard.

The revolver dropped beside the oracle's corpse. Danny leaned against the dog, still waiting, still whining, and wrapped his arms around the animal as more and more approaching sirens erupted across the night sky. He squeezed the dog, burying his face into its warm fur, and the tears dried, his mind as emptied as the handgun.

"You're a good boy," he said. "Good, lucky boy. Lucky, lucky boy, Charlie."

The dog slid out from between his clenched arms, glanced around at the hollow bodies, and stepped through the door, into the cool evening air. Danny didn't protest, didn't call out, didn't claw the floor in vain for its return.

"That's a good boy," he repeated, letting the poison settle; a grin pulled across his face by the hands of unknowable certainty. "Lucky boy."

# THE LIMITATIONS OF SEAGULLS

*"a seabird knew your name"* – Tim Buckley

**M.J. Arcangelini**

The seagulls did know your name, but
Like telemarketers and receptionists
They found it difficult to pronounce.
That is why, as they circled above the
Picnic table eyeing our sandwiches,
Everything they said sounded like
Squawking and you could never tell
Whether they were addressing you
Directly or simply commenting on the
Weather, the size of the waves crashing
Against the beach boulders, their cold
Hungry lust for your lunch and mine.
Then, the wandering albatross arrived.

# Adelita

## Gwil James Thomas

I've never been to New York City
and perhaps I never will –
but I've been with a New Yorker.

She was a Mexican American
from Spanish Harlem –
I'd met her when I was drunk
and mentioned meeting again
so that I could practice my Spanish –
the *'Spanish classes,'* always ended up
with me drunk, her high, after which
we'd fuck and speak English anyway.

She'd tell me about growing up
in Spanish Harlem and I'd tell her
about the places that I'd lived in –
in truth, there wasn't much between us
besides the fact that we were both
two strangers far from our homes.

But one morning I remember her

waking me from my sleep with a kiss,

before she said, *'I just wanna make you happy,'*

perhaps it was the fact that I'd woken up

too early, but something about it had

moved me in a way that I hadn't expected

and I wondered what else she had to say

that could captivate me in such a distinct way,

as she then slid her hand down my face

and ever so softly whispered –

*'I want you to cum on my tits.'*

# A Broken Heart

Gwil James Thomas

Brought with it a lot,

mostly god awful poems

like this –

that were only written,

because in the end even

a poem plucked

from a broken heart's

pus filled crust

was a true gift,

compared to anything else,

it had left to offer.

# Vigilante

Aimee Nicole

Throw secrets in
the washing machine—
watch all the lies spill out,
bang against the door for freedom.
Every marriage is full
of revenge, anniversaries
built on endings.
All that remains is dust,
remnants of who
we were meant to become.

# UVA /B Rays

## Aimee Nicole

And when I'm pinned beneath you,

just know I'm omniscient like a sun glare...

patiently waiting for the bend.

I'll inch so cleverly into your vision

and obstruct everything you once saw so clear.

# Anonymity

## William Barker

The familiar bell of his favorite liquor store jingled when Bukowski pulled open the door. It had been weeks since he stepped foot in here. Lately the bars grabbed him again which meant too much money out of pocket and too many human beings surrounding him. He needed some solitude. A good, long weekend, alone. No phone calls. No visitors. Today he was running a bit behind schedule, having gotten caught up in important things at the racetrack. If he wanted to make it home and start writing at his old Post Office punch-in time, as was the ritual, he needed to hurry.

"What's happening, Hank?" Joe asked, using a nickname Bukowski reserved only for his closest cohorts. Joe paused briefly from stocking red wine. "You rich and famous yet?"

Hank paused, his heavy brow raising as he smiled slightly before answering, "Still a servant. Now instead of the post office it's these god damn magazines and publications. Hardly even gets the rent and child support, man."

Joe smiled showing several missing teeth and nodded. "I've got four kids, man. You're preaching to the choir." He said, folding up some cardboard. "You'll do it Hank and when you do, don't forget good ol' Joe."

"Course I won't, baby." Hank said. "You just keep supplying the booze and I'll keep stabbing at the dream with this broken knife."

Joe laughed and Hank walked away, turning down another isle. He really never knew the drink he came for specifically, just that he needed to stock up to encourage whatever the creative act had available for him over the weekend. Like with food or women, an alcoholic sometimes goes through phases, or at least he did. Some months it's wine, others whiskey, though lately he'd been drinking a lot of beer again. He headed to the refrigerated section, its shelves filled top to bottom with cans and bottles of beer with colorful labels and interesting logos. Hank grabbed two sixes of Miller, made his way towards the counter and put them down. A whole weekend alone, what a refreshing thought. He closed his eyes a second, picturing the thump of his typer knocking out poems to the accompaniment of some fantastic classical music. Write, sleep, wake up, repeat, repeat. No human infiltration. None. His adrenaline increased and a selfish smile parted his lips. He decided to grab two bottles of Vodka along with a couple two liters of 7-UP. These, the beer, and the bottles of red wine back at this apartment, should do the trick, giving him enough for the whole weekend without another run to Old Joe's.

The boy behind the counter kept his eyes low, ringing up the beer, then the Vodka and soda. Hank absently wondered if the kid was even old enough to buy liquor, let alone sell it. After slipping the glass bottles of hard liquor into thin paper bags the kid mumbled, "That will be three bucks, sir" like a dying parrot. Hank reached into his pocket, pulled out his wallet and removed three one's. He heard the jingle of the front door again as he handed the money over, followed by the cash register bell chiming before it opened. Soon there was a shuffle of feet behind him, and some grunting. When several bottles smashed on the ground, Hank, a bit startled, turned sluggishly towards the noise. A man wearing a gray ski mask, holding a shotgun, shoved Joe down an isle towards the register.

"You, behind the counter, get up in front with the other guy. Everyone on the ground!" The robber shouted, heaving Joe forward. Hank, feeling pretty buzzed, felt befuddled a moment and didn't react. "What are you waiting for old man?" The robber said to him, "Get on the ground, this is a fucking stick-up!"

The beers at the track left him feeling pretty daring. Hank's brow furrowed, begrudgingly he acquiesced, lowering to a crouch, but found himself unable to resist a wise crack. "Only time I get down like this is to take a big shit." Hank stammered.

"I don't remember telling anyone they could speak." The robber shrieked through his gray ski mask. Before Hank could even react, the gunman held a handful of his collar. "Shut the fuck up old man and get down on your stomach like the boy did." He pointed at Joe and yelled, "You, get the god damned money out of the register, all of it! I know you're the owner of this place so don't pull any shit."

"Okay, okay." Joe bumbled, waving his hands in the air. "I'm not gonna pull any shit. I have a wife and kids—

"Don't care. Just get the fucking money." His attention returned to Hank who still wasn't lying down. Jamming the gun directly into Hank's chest in disbelief, he shouted, "That's it, old man, if you don't get the fuck down on the floor, I'm going to have to spray whatever is left of your hero guts all over that poor cashier down there. Have

47

you ever seen what a shotgun does to a human being? Mincemeat, old man..."

"Just get down, Hank, Jesus." Joe screamed, gathering the cash in a fat stack. The gunmen let the gun sag slightly and cocked his head in Hank's direction like a stupid dog might at its owner.

"Did you say, Hank?" The robber asked Joe, who didn't answer.

Still on his knees Hank mused, "You know, this would make for a damn good story. Only thing is, I have to survive to actually write the words down." He put his arms out in front of him, the palms of his hands facing up. "What do you say, man? I'll make you look really fucking macho with an American story of desperation and everything..." Hank pulled his upper lip back and showed some teeth. "I'm a writer, man...I can do anything. I'm God on the page."

The robber lowered the gun completely. "It is you!" He tore off his mask and stuffed it in his coat pocket. He couldn't have been more than twenty years old. "You're Charles Bukowski." He wagged an index finger in the air at Hank. "I know it's you. I saw you read at Cal. State..."

Joe slammed the wad of money on the counter.

"This is all that's in the register," he said in a huff. "Here, just take it..."

Carefully the shotgun went back up as the robber moved to snatch up the money.

Now dealing with a fan of his work, Hank felt even more gutsy and confident. He got to his feet slowly and tucked the bottom of his white button-down shirt over his gut and back into the waist of his pants. "You're a fan, huh?" He said in a dry tone. "And a gun pointed at me is appreciation, I'm guessing? That would be like me spitting in Hemingway's whiskey before passing him the fucking glass."

The gunman nodded. "A fan, for sure. I've got a few of your earlier books, but mostly I've read you in the magazines." His eyes were like a starstruck teenage girl on the red carpet in Hollywood. "I want to write like you someday. I've had a crazy life, too. I grew up poor, fucked up family situation, and all of that..."

"And the gun pointed at me?" Hank repeated.

"Yeah, sorry about that. My nerves are peaked and I didn't recognize you at first..."

Hank extended an index finger towards the barrel. "It's still pointed at me, baby. I'm starting to sweat here."

49

The robber finally lowered his gun. "Hey, despite all of this, do you think I can get an autograph?" He begged.

Joe came out from behind the counter. "Can you leave my store? You've already got what you came for..."

Hank put a hand out to silence the store owner. "Hey, Joe, can you get me a piece of paper and something to write on?"

"You're really going to give this guy an autograph?" Joe asked. "He just robbed me!"

Hank shrugged. "He is a fan, Joe. Can you get me the damned paper and pen?" To the robber he asked, "What's your name, man?"

"Eddie." The gunmen said.

Instead of just an autograph, Hank wrote him one of his trademark little notes, complete with cartoon artwork that read like this:

*Edward, thanks for making me feel alive today. Whatever is going on in your life, work it out, man. By the way, that shotgun pointed at me really killed my buzz. You owe me a bottle! -Charles Bukowski*

The gunmen snatched the paper like a schoolboy with his first crush. "Thanks, Hank!" He lowered his gaze to his toes. "Can I call you, Hank?"

"Sure, baby. You're the one with the gun." Hank quipped. "So, we good now?" Eddie nodded. "Okay, good. Don't ever bother Joe again, he is a good man and his stuff keeps the words coming." Hank pointed a parental finger at him. "You want me to keep writing, right?" The kid nodded again. "Good, so don't come in here ever again."

"Okay." He raised the autographed note into the air like a trophy and planted a long kiss onto it. "Thanks again, Hank!" He shouted over his shoulder, bolting towards the door.

Soon the bell jingled and the robber was gone. Joe immediately called the police to report the crime. After slamming the phone down, Joe huffed and puffed, "I can't believe you gave him what he wanted, Hank. That little shit didn't deserve it!"

"Put your hand on your heart, Joe. Is it beating?" Hank waited a few seconds, after Joe nodded and shrugged, he finished, "Yeah, that's what I thought. It was the best choice given the circumstances..."

"You're right." Joe admitted, finally. "Thank you, Hank." He extended a hand, which Hank immediately shook. His face gravely serious, Joe said, "In my day a handshake meant sincerity. Don't underestimate it, my friend."

"I won't, Joe. Not a chance." Hank said.

The cashier boy got to his feet and dusted himself off, his face pale as skim milk. "You can go home after the police take the report." Joe told him.

"I'm glad I came in here today," Hank put an elbow on the counter, "now I have something to write about until the booze kicks in and brings me the muse."

"Could have turned out much worse." Joe declared, walking over to the shelf to grab a bottle. "Hey, I need a shot of something, how about you?"

"You buying?" Hank asked.

"Why not," Joe muttered with a shrug. "I just got cleaned out, what's a little more..."

They shared a shot of some damn good Bourbon and then two more. Joe finally broke the silence by asking,

"Hank, was it scary having that huge gun pointed directly at you?"

Without hesitation Hank blurted, "What bothered me more is that the fucker recognized me..."

"Wait, what?" Joe asked, obviously very confused.

"He recognized me, baby. Means my anonymity is completely gone now." Hank poured himself a fourth shot of Bourbon and downed it. "Looks like I'm on my way..."

"How the hell is that a bad thing, Hank?" He asked.

"Because, Joe," Hank asserted. "I can't stand people. Now I get the feeling they'll never leave me alone again."

# Night Alone

Paul Cordeiro

1.)

night alone inside the world of a book

ad free

2.)

roughing penalty:

cross-cut to a head bouncing

off-road work truck ad

3.)

the concussed QB

stumbles with knees wobbly;

goes into the game

on the next drive an adman

for Eveready

# Seafood Faux Pas

Paul Cordeiro

sending back
lightly cooked tuna;
his friend's raw laughter

# Blood Feud

## Eddie Black

Grant took a hit from a pint of Old Tub and flipped on the headlights as he pulled off of the road and aimed his truck into the woods, crawling over the juts and ditching. A few more swallows would usher in nightfall and he spent the next forty-five minutes drinking and looking at the dying timber and had not seen a single animal, not that he had been looking for one. He glazed through the Kentucky bourbon and then into whatever remained in a round flask he had spotted in the floorboards of the passenger side. Might have been chicha left behind from Paz, a Chilean with whom he spent a few easy months with and then a half as many hellish ones before she hopped a Greyhound to somewhere younger. He wedged the open flask in between the armrest of the bench seat. Nipping from it and returning it whenever the urge arose.

He drank with intent but was never sure what the intention was. It had been this way since his first boyhood taste. Angry at the world. At his situation. At himself for being born into a situation where he had needed to drink angrily and often. When you came from the womb already a failure it seemed as if the world had you labeled from the moment it saw you first and wasn't in the business of reneging on the deal. His mother had also defecated on him during the delivery and he was javelina angry about that as well, as he seldom accepted an omen graciously.

When Grant was out of the mystery liquid he tossed the flask out the window for no other reason than to do it and decided to head to wetter ground. He put the truck into gear but before he took his foot off the brake, a black squirrel landed directly on his hood. Grant jumped in his seat. The squirrel moved in short scrambling bursts. It made its way around the sun damaged hood in crescent like routes and stopped only once to stare him directly in the eyes, neither one of them wavering. The growing ash began to lay waste to the Lucky Strike he held in his big lips and the smoldering started to irritate his gin blossom. The entire situation began to unnerve him slightly for a moment and then not at all. He reversed back out onto the main road without checking his mirrors, watching the squirrel jump from the hood onto the ground in a black blur.

He wanted beer. The liquors did not blend as well as he had hoped and were reacting badly with the spansule of speed he had taken. He figured a light beer and then a dark beer could settle it. If not he would burn the joint he had stashed behind his right ear, which would do it, or at least level it off for another spansule. Rock and roll science he called it.

There were three watering holes in town. The Redroom Inn, where anyone who knew better never bought a room on account of a bed bug infestation and the ghost in Room 2, but where the bar was alright. Then there was Midy's, and the Ündercliffte, which was a three-sided bar built into the side of the bluff.

He had gotten kicked out of Midy's last Wednesday and was taking a short leave from there while things cooled down and was closest to Redroom Inn anyway so that's where he decided to go. His perpetual anger had simmered to about the lowest it gets and the blurred drive was nicer than wood watching.

One of life's simple pleasures was buzzed driving. Now the bastards from the big cities were going to get that taken from us as well with their national commercial campaigns showing pictures of roadside wreckage. Who the hell wanted to see that while they were trying to eat their supper? Besides, no one who lived rurally ever got killed from driving buzzed or blind drunk even. A dented bumper maybe. Or you had to repair someone's fence for them or bury a dog once you sobered up, but that was about the extent of it. Before too long you wouldn't be able to do anything anymore. We'll be just like Canada. Or Illinois.

The six parking spots in front of the Redroom were filled with trucks as well as four motorcycles on the outside of them. Three Harleys on one side, a Suzuki on the other, where it was less apt to get kicked over or pissed on, yet not completely in the clear.

Grant took one look at the green Chevrolet in the third spot and knew who it was that called it theirs. He knew that when the ignition was on the belt screamed and the brakes screamed. He could hear it without even trying. He knew he shouldn't go in. He was turning fifty-one this upcoming spring and Lee would be fifty himself. He didn't know how much longer they could keep this up, but he was also going to be damned if that egg sucking dog was going to stand in the way of him getting a drink in his place of birth, the place he had been raised and lived, and the place where he would eventually be buried.

He tried to remember when it had started. He had taken Lee's left eye when they were in Junior High, but it had started before that. He thought on it and chewed his tongue. It came back as clear as if it had been a black squirrel on his hood.

He had been raised in a family of twelve children, all less than a year apart, which really just meant they had been raised poor and that the doorknob to their parent's bedroom was often tube socked. They would round up all the kids twice a week to attend church. Middling kids sitting on the olderns' laps and the youngest laid in between the floorboards, crying usually. His parents never even owned a bible except the one from the Samaritan's that Daddy held when panhandling and it was hollered out to hold his cash, but low-income members of the congregation got free canned goods regularly and oftentimes a few dollars slipped in between handshakes from a dozen members or so who took pity on them for having all those kids and no prospects.

Lee was raised a lot less hungry than Grant, which caused a bit of animosity in its own right, but he remembered the exact date he hated him first. Lee's father was a dentist and had a taste for expensive horses and his mother was an artist on a hot streak, the type of which got their works bought before they were finished and shown at Universities and fairs. The entire town treated her like she was some sort of homebred celebrity. Grant didn't understand it himself. Her paintings all just looked like pussies to him. She had one in particular that looked like a broken horse's leg that got her tossed out of the church, but before that, once a year she would donate all the clothes that Lee and his sister had outgrown.

Grant had shown up to Sunday School wearing a little denim jacket lined with wool she had donated and in front of the whole class Lee started screaming at him. "That's my jacket! You stole my jacket! That's mine!" All the children looked at Grant with those big eyes they had always aimed at him differently and his siblings differently than those of them who had never known hunger or hand me downs. He wanted to cry and to fight them all. He was stung with embarrassment and he yanked the jacket off and threw it in the screaming face of Lee. Even now in remembrance he was white knuckling the steering wheel. When you were poor you never got over the unloving feeling of inadequacy.

Lee's old man ended up getting kicked in the head and hemorrhaging in their stable and his family started to lose everything from the debt of their lifestyle and without any money coming in from the dentistry or from his mother's vagina paintings, which her fifteen minutes had been up on, they fell on hard times as well. Lee had begun to get just as angry at the world as Grant had always been and all they ever had to take it out on was each other and themselves, doing a great many horrible things over the years, each outing seemingly more life changing than the next.

Grant stared at the truck and managed his hate. If it had been even three years prior he already would have put the front end of his truck into the back end of Lee's, but he wasn't three years younger and time had a way of changing certain things outright, or at least the way you thought about them. But there simply wasn't much else to do and never was. He slammed the door behind him and scraped his shit kickers off on the concrete.

The closer he got, the madder he got. Thinking of all the times Lee had bested him. When he had been put into a coma from a table leg to the back of the head, losing two months of his life and coming back only to find out that his wife had taken a turn for the worse and had died while he had been under. When they had run into each other deer hunting on public land and had a brief bolt action gun fight, Grant losing most of his left thumb and his only rifle. He hadn't been able to hunt for six years now because of Lee, let alone play darts anymore and he had relied heavily on those winnings to settle the monthly bills.

He walked through the doors and scanned the room for that big oaken fool. His hands were balled into fists and his lips were tucked into his mouth. Lee was nowhere to be found. He was angry at his relief. Lee must have gotten drunk here yesterday and left his truck out front and hadn't been back to get it. Probably sleeping one off.

He sat at the bar in front of Shelbie Dysktra, who was acting a mite strange but she was a mite strange and he thought very little about it. He ordered two beers from her and asked her how she had been. She tried to speak but only chirped nervously as she popped the caps from the bottles and sat them in front of him.

A door slammed near the pool tables, which is where the bathroom was, and everyone that was in the Redroom bar made their way to the walls in complete silence. Shelbie Dykstra wheezed and recoiled into herself. Grant turned on the stool and faced Lee who was drying his hands with a paper towel. His black patch crooked against his head. When the eyes met the eye, the room changed. When the wet paper towel hit the floor, Grant came off of his stool. It was silent for an entire song. They were old and they were big and they hated.

Lee snatched the cue ball from the snooker table and flung it across the room where Grant ducked and it smashed directly into the neck of Shelbie Dykstra who collapsed with a choking honk. Grant grabbed the necks of each beer bottle. The damaged thumb's bottle flew wildly off target but the other landed against Lee who deflected the blow with a boxer's parry. He was covered in cheap beer and angry about it and angry at horses that kicked dentists and that there was a dribble of urine down his leg even though he had shaken it six times or more.

They met in the middle and were bleeding profusely after the very first combinations. Lee had him clinched and Grant worked his thumb up Lee's twisted face and slipped it under his eye patch and into the socket beneath it. Lee creaked like a felled tree and let his enemy loose, pushing him in the chest and getting a short distance between them. They were both wheezing for air, when Lee began to pelt Grant with little pink snooker balls. He covered up and grunted in pain with each womp. He drove his forearm into the ditch of Lee's neck, smashing it with multiple wet slaps.

Neither man blocked a shot but fought back with their own strikes, taking extreme damage and dealing an uncontrollable amount of rage and past receipts with each given blow. Grant had turned Lee around and was trying to get a sleeper hold applied, but Lee put his hand against the wall and donkey kicked him three feet across the second pool table.

Lee leapt over the table to meet him, staggering on a few billiards, and when he came down Grant caught him squarely on the front of his chin and his lights dimmed. There was panic in him and he knew he was in trouble. The lights went out and when they came on again, his back was on the green felt and Grant was choking him to death. He clawed at the gnarled fingers at his neck but there was no strength to him.

No one in the bar moved as Grant killed Lee. They watched coldly or in fear or with the notion that these two men had been heading this direction for years. Grant felt victory in his blood and began laughing like a murder of crows and he tightened his grip centimeter by centimeter. He was sweating from his back and arms and he felt an ice cube slide wetly across his belly. When he coughed, his guts fell out of him. A puff of warm fumes wafted between him and Lee and into his face.

He let go of the throat and caught his intestines, trying to push them back into himself as Lee collapsed onto the floor gasping and hacking phlegm, a scarlet filet knife in his red right hand. His head bounced on the floor as he heaved and pushed himself by his boots under the table and away from Grant who was whispering the name of his childhood dog over and over.

Grant held his guts in his hands and stumbled across the bar and out the doors, leaking over it all. The air was cold and what was fire-hot in his hands moments before, was only warm now. His feet scooted across the ground and he felt like a stack of dirty dishes trying to balance on butterknife legs. The clinic was two miles east. He could make it.

As he shuffled across the ground all of the thoughts he had ever had of the memories he had left hit the center of his self like a Missouri tornado. Few of them were good and he felt shame. All of the faces he had made while warring with the world played in his mind close enough to smell and he was scared. He saw all of the times he had battled Lee and all the times he had lost and won and the times he hadn't remembered were now laid in front of him like the photographs of his ancestors and their children and their deaths.

He fell to his knees on the road and now all his mind could conjure was Lee. They had been the only two people there for each other in their lives, and yes they hated each other but so what? Maybe they hadn't been honorable men or even good men, but they had both known where the other lived and slept and worked and had never taken it there, and that was something.

He bent in the middle and touched his forehead to the cold road. A pebble bit into him. He could no longer hold open his eyes and he knew his hands were about to fail him as well. There was his breathing. Slow and loud and unpowerful. There was the sound of a church organ and slamming doors. Then there was only his breath again. Slow. Quieter now. Then was the sound of a truck approaching from behind. The belt screamed. The brakes screamed.

# Karen Goes to Woodstock

John Dorsey

& not quite thirteen

you cry out

in the middle

of a rainy afternoon

for a girl you haven't met

dancing on wet grass

leaves pressed tight

up against her thighs

the wind is a song

that you hum

about the future

when you don't know

exactly

where your scream

will land.

# Up To Here Waiting For Us I Think

Steve Zmijewski

Cold feet ashake atop older tile,

my back exposed in an off-green gown.

Wind shoves skinny tree appendages,

the branches slap the screened window of the room I am in.

I look out through this funnel,

shortsighted,

imagining an angel from an ancient stage ballet dancing

upon misshapen hooves. They appear as

torches with sling hooks singeing and

shredding it all.

Cherry blossom leaves plunge like loose leaf paper,

twigs like ruptured tentacles.


Overhead, a dented speaker tells me

a five day forecast that means n o t h i n g

to this mess in my head,

crawling my skin, redding my eyes.

Not allowing myself to blink.

How many more times will someone say

*it feels like January,*

when it isn't. When

I don't want to feel anything
other than whatever better means to you.
And I don't want to know anything
other than escape from the absurdity
I think we deserve -

bodies burning
on the underside of our fading sun.

# FUCK MACHINE

**Bradford Middleton**

I was like a fuck machine
Just waiting to happen and
There was this one lucky lady
Who I was going to fuck
Until Kingdom come or
Probably just me and
When she realised this
She dumped me for one
Date with an old landlord

From there she moved on
To another, each becoming more
Androgynous than the last
Until one came along
A man who'd become a woman
We carried on as friends
And one weekend when away
At an upmarket festival I returned

Our chalet is where I saw it
And my eyes went askew
My poor brain needed drowning

There she was being fucked in

Her arse by a strap-on that

Put anything I could ever

Muster to puny little shame

So I went out and got

Drunk for three nights and two days

Until our return home to London town

# I Hate My Life

Jason Gerrish

We sat in the heated company van,
waiting on DC; Wade glared at the ice,
the dirty slush that buried the road.

"Jerk me off," he said.
"My hands are rough," I told him.
"So?" he said, "Just pull on it a little."

I cracked the window to smoke, asked Wade
"How long since you got some from your neighbor?"
He rolled his eyes, turned away. "What?" I said.
"She's dead," said Wade, and after some prying,
he told me how it happened.

"We fucked a few times, and it was fine,
but she started coming over every night, so,
I broke it off, and the next morning, her
daughter's car was parked in her drive,
with the ambulance and the coroner's vehicle."

"How old was she?" I said.

"Just 50," said Wade.

"You broke her heart," I said.

"Shut up, Stupid."


I said, "If she stayed that night,

she'd have died in your bed."

"I know," said Wade,

glared at the snow. Then,

"Where the fuck is DC?

I hate my life."

# Its a Wonderful Wife

Danny D Ford

flipping out
is embarrassing
and necessary

there's only
so much face
a grown man
can save
while stomping
on an empty
frozen
pizza box
screaming
WHAT'S FUCKING
WRONG WITH YOU?

love
is a tiny
yellow blossom
gone

in a moment's breeze

when I repeat
in my head
*till death do us part*
*till death do us part*
lucifer lets out a little laugh
cats look confused
& a hairline
somewhere
recedes

steel railway lines wish
they were as sturdy
as her tiny nod

the nod
that means
*not a fucking chance*

# Bonnie Parker Heart

Jason Baldinger

I've been dragging this cold front
over three scarecrow states
all I want is a decent meal
                    a decent beer

greeted by axel
I wonder briefly why
a seven year old boy
is seated at the bar solo

with the expense of childcare
wouldn't be strange
he's the server's kid
crayon drawn menus
'til shifts end

it wouldn't be strange
his family are regulars
axel wanted to sit by himself
independent or willful

or maybe this youngin'
has a crush on the bartender
her tight autumn sweater
drenched in a volume of curls

a man next to axel
tosses soft voiced questions
as axel tries for the gold
asks the bartender
to fry him a steak

my food arrives
with cops behind me
they use *gentle* cop voices
axel's mother is looking for him

axel is defiant
cops corral him
into a squad car
boy convict
swept up in a sting
a crown of priors
to break a bartender's
bonnie parker heart

# The High and Hundred Proof Choir

Jason Baldinger

legs hang from a sky
choked out in deep black
it's threatened since dayton
hang on hydroplane
the buckets come
other side of the state line

this bar is overrun with roughnecks
road crew yellow shirts stained
evening happy hour spirals into night

slurs, bravado
exchange punches across the bar
these working man's things

blonde secretary runs the jukebox
senior prom hits
from a decade ago
back when day jobs
were nightmares

only parents talked about

outside it's howling
a road crew knows
each drink that takes today's pain
starts tomorrow's deficit

they fall off stools
into autopilot drunk drives
into bed, as they muster
they whisper a prayer to weather

I'll pray tonight
with the high and hundred proof choir
let the rain come
let the jobs and roads wash away
let us all sleep deep into the infinity
of an unexpected three-day weekend
these savored gifts
braced against a hangovers pain

# Yellow

Jonathan S Baker

filmed walls

flushed bowels

crusted bowl

sick water

flop sweat

limp tissue

paper thin

cowardice

shriveled

psychosis

cum dribble

shamed

Van Gogh

paints my bath

## WOODY HARRELSON

My great grandmother fell backward into
his arms while going up the stairs at a casino
in Las Vegas years ago, and years after that
my older brother met him and complained
to me that he was stoned, which only confirms
my long held argument that stoners save lives.

## PEST

a kid
I live with
asked me
why I look tired
all of the time
and I told him
it was because
of his youth

# Resolution

Joseph Fulkerson

*I love the noises made during battle.*
*The sound that's created when I draw my sword.*
*When it strikes another.*
*When I cut through flesh and bone, muscle and sinew.*
*The lopping sound when taking the head of my enemy.*
*The warm, crimson geyser of arterial spray.*
*The sights, sounds, and smell of battle are all incredibly gratifying.*

*Yet none of them compare to the sound my sword makes going*
*into its sheath.*
*That is the sound of resolution. The sound of finality.*
*It's the freedom cry that draws me into battle.*

*There will come a day my adversary experiences this instead.*
*I will fall by his hand.*
*It will be an honorable death.*
*But not today.*

*As the sun sets on this day, I stand ready for the next duel.*

# Contributors

in order of appearance